HUMAN LIVING SYSTEMS

The Immune System

WITHDRAWN

KAREN BLEDSOE

LLOYDMINSTER PUBLIC LIBRARY

PERFECTION LEARNING®

Editorial Director: Susan C. Thies
Editor: Mary L. Bush
Design Director: Randy Messer
Book Design: Tobi S. Cunningham, Lori Gould, Robin Elwick
Cover Design: Michael Aspengren

A special thanks to the following for his scientific review of the book:
Paul Pistek, Instructor of Biological Sciences,
North Iowa Area Community College

Image credits:
©ISM/PhototakeUSA.com: pp. 5 (left), 11 (top); ©Visuals Unlimited/Corbis: pp. 14, 16 (bottom), 18 (bottom); ©Jean Claude Revy–ISU/PhototakeUSA.com: p. 15; ©Lester V. Bergman/CORBIS: pp. 16 (top), 16–17 (background); ©Mediscan/Corbis: p. 17 (top); ©Eddie Adams/Sygma/Corbis: p. 23

photos.com: all left/right page backgrounds, pp. 9 (bottom), 10, 11 (bottom), 21, 24, 26 (bottom), 29 (right), 34 (top), 35 (right); istockphoto.com: covers, pp. 1, 2–3, 4, 5 (right), 6–7 (background), 7, 9 (top), 11 (middle), 12, 13, 20, 22 (bottom), 25, 27, 29 (left), 30–31 (background), 31, 32, 34–35 (background), 36, 37; phil.cdc.gov: pp. 26 (top), 33, 40; PLC: pp. 6, 8, 18 (top), 19, 22 (top), 28

Text © 2007 by Perfection Learning® Corporation.
All rights reserved. No part of this book may be reproduced, stored in a retrieval system, or transmitted in any form or by any means, electronic, mechanical, photocopying, recording, or otherwise, without prior permission of the publisher. Printed in the United States of America.

For information, contact
Perfection Learning® Corporation
1000 North Second Avenue, P.O. Box 500
Logan, Iowa 51546-0500.
Phone: 1-800-831-4190
Fax: 1-800-543-2745
perfectionlearning.com

1 2 3 4 5 6 PP 12 11 10 09 08 07

PB ISBN 0-7891-7019-1
RLB ISBN 0-7569-6644-2

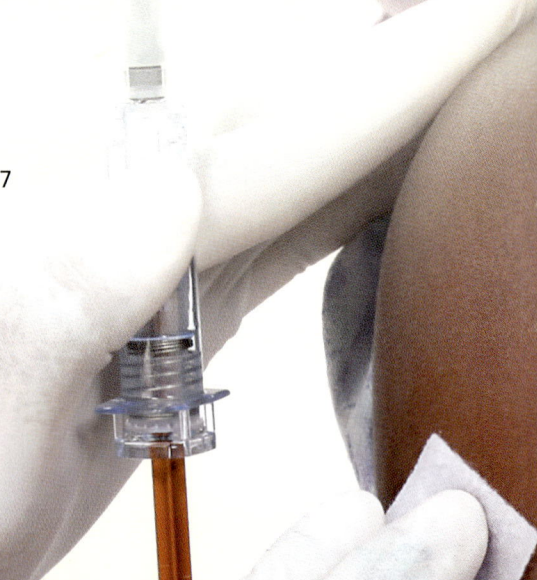

Table of Contents

1. A System of Defense 4
2. Putting Up Barriers 10
3. Attack and Defend 13
4. Immunization: Helping Out the Immune System 20
5. Breakdowns in the System 24
6. New Investigations into the Immune System 30
Internet Connections for the Immune System 37
Glossary 38
Index 40

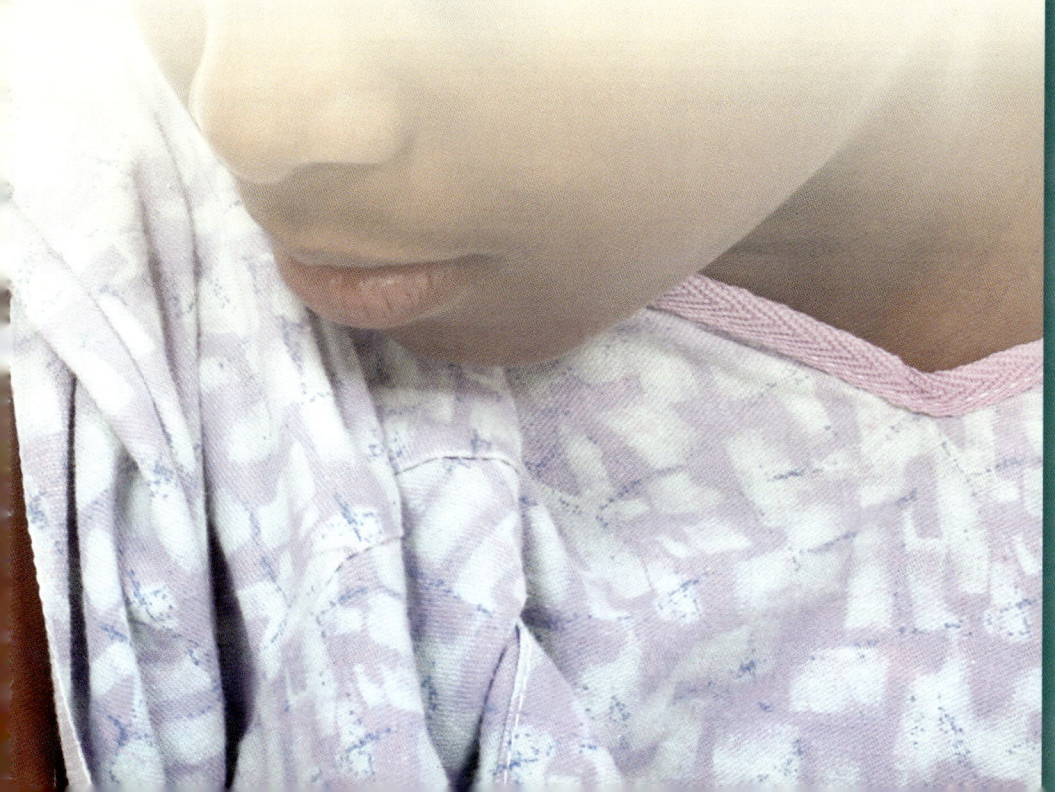

chapter one

A System of Defense

Millions of tiny bodies surround you every day. They swarm around you in the air, rest on surfaces you touch, and live on and in your food. Sound scary? It's not really. Most of these hovering bodies are harmless. Some are even helpful to you. Only a few can cause problems if they get inside. How does your body defend you against these potential invaders? It relies on your immune system.

The Immune System

Your immune system is a group of **cells, tissues,** and **organs** that work together to keep invaders out and destroy those that do get in. The immune system also keeps track of past intruders and makes substances to fight them off if they return. The members of the immune system include the lymphatic vessels, lymph nodes, red bone marrow, white blood cells, thymus gland, spleen, appendix, adenoids, tonsils, and Peyer's patches. Each of these parts plays an important role in your body's defense.

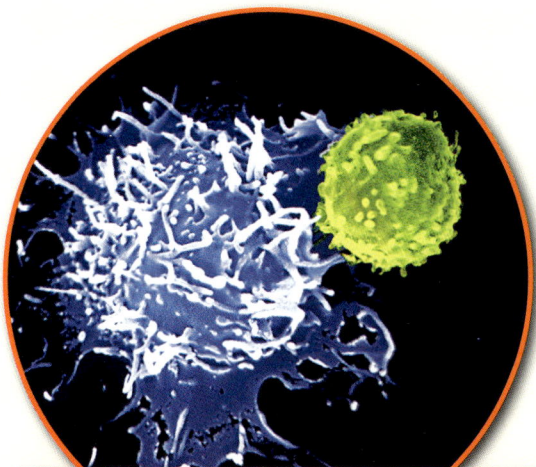

An antigen-presenting cell (blue) interacts with a type of white blood cell known as a T cell (green)

Antigen Alert!

Antigens are responsible for determining whether a substance belongs to a specific body or not. Antigens are chemical identification markers present on both substances that do and don't belong to a body. When an antigen indicates that something doesn't belong, the immune system steps in to get rid of it.

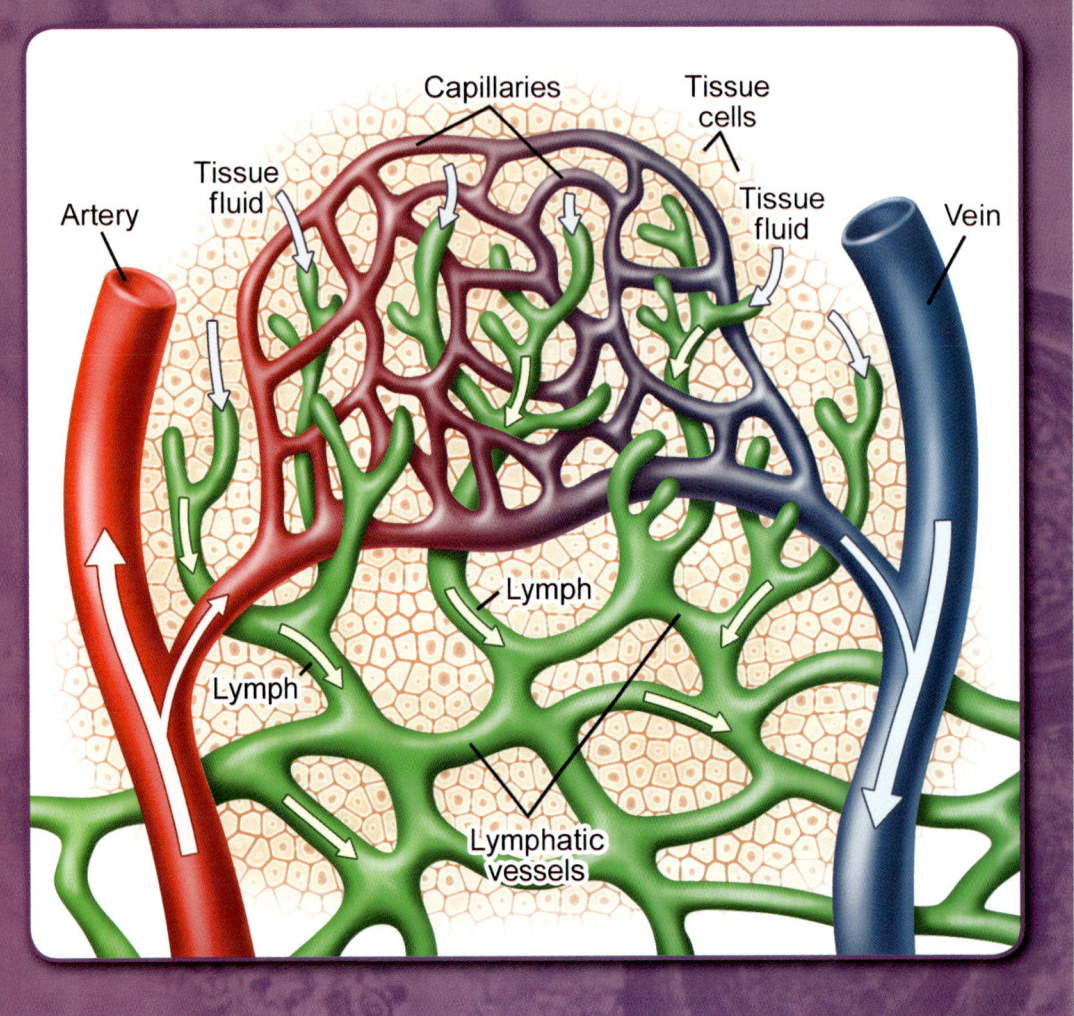

The **lymphatic vessels** help return excess tissue fluid back to the bloodstream. This extra fluid was left behind during the exchange of nutrients and waste. Once the fluid enters the lymphatic vessels, it's called *lymph*. On the trip back to the blood, the lymph is filtered by the **lymph nodes**. These nodes remove cellular debris and foreign bodies such as **bacteria**. After the waste and bacteria have been removed by the lymph nodes, the "clean" lymph is sent out to the body again.

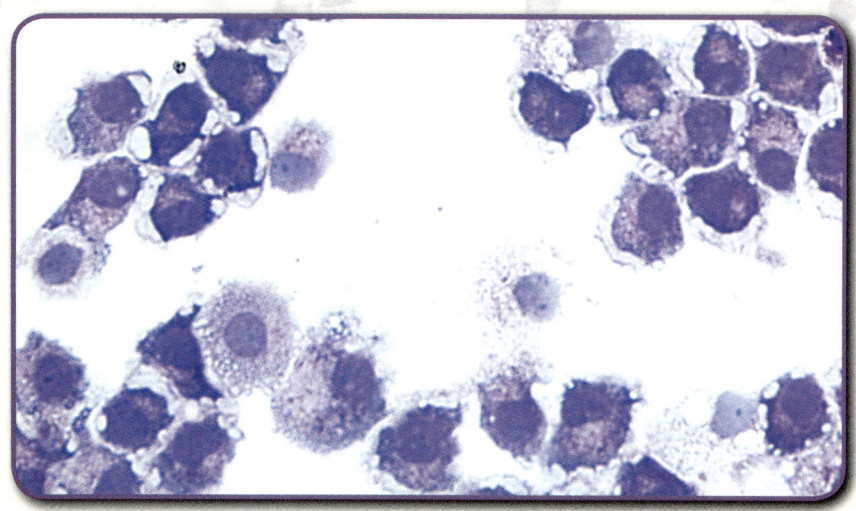

White blood cells

Red bone marrow is found in many bones. This bone marrow produces **stem cells**. These stem cells can divide to produce several different types of cells, including red and **white blood cells**. White blood cells play a key role in chasing down and destroying **pathogens** in the body.

Bacteria cells

Pathogens Can Cause Suffering!

A pathogen is any disease-causing agent. The word *pathogen* comes from the Greek word *pathos*, which means "suffering" or "disease." Pathogens include bacteria, **viruses**, fungi, and parasites such as tapeworms.

In babies, some of the white blood cells travel to the **thymus gland**, a small organ near the heart. In the thymus, the cells mature into **T cells** that are specially trained to recognize which cells belong to a body and to destroy those that don't. Scientists have not discovered any important role for the thymus in adults.

The **spleen** is the largest lymphoid organ in the body. The spleen's responsibilities are almost identical to those of the lymph nodes, except that the spleen filters all of the blood, not just the lymph. The spleen also removes old red blood cells and stores new ones. This is why the spleen is a reddish color.

The appendix, adenoids, tonsils, and Peyer's patches are made of lymphoid tissues. These areas help the lymphatic system get rid of unwanted invaders.

The Immune System

- Adenoids
- Tonsils
- Thymus gland
- Lymph nodes
- Lymphatic vessels
- Spleen
- Peyer's patches
- Lymph nodes
- Appendix
- Red bone marrow
- Lymphatic vessels

Losing Parts of the Immune System

Sometimes people must have their spleens, appendixes, or tonsils removed due to an accident, infection, or constant illness. People can live without these organs because other parts of the immune system will take over. However, in the case of a lost spleen, they may get sick more often.

Immunity Is Important

The immune system is designed to provide you with **immunity** to the pathogens you encounter. Immunity is a body's ability to resist illnesses, diseases, or infections. The stronger your immunity, the healthier you are.

To keep your immunity strong, it's important to eat right, exercise, get enough rest, and control your stress. When you're tired and run-down, your immune system is weakened, making it possible for tricky invaders to get past your defenses and attack. Doing your part to support your immune system will give you the power of immunity!

chapter two

Putting Up Barriers

To avoid getting a sunburn, you might wear a hat or sunscreen to shield you from the Sun. The human body uses the same strategy to keep pathogens out. The body has several barriers that block harmful trespassers from getting in.

Skin is the largest of these barriers. Dead skin cells on the surface of the skin form a tight shield that pathogens have a hard time penetrating. Dead cells are constantly flaking off, carrying potential invaders with them. Friendly bacteria live in the cracks in skin, crowding out disease-causing pathogens.

Cilia lining the lungs

The mucous membranes that line the mouth, nose, lungs, stomach, and intestines also fight off pathogens. The sticky mucus that lines these tissues traps pathogens, preventing them from traveling farther inside the body to reproduce. Cells in the lungs have extensions called *cilia* that sweep mucus out, carrying pathogens with it.

Several fluids in the body also keep pathogens from doing damage. Saliva, sweat, and tears destroy certain types of bacteria. All three also wash away destructive intruders. Strong acids in the stomach kill bacteria that make it that far.

Inquire and Investigate
Skin As a Barrier

Question: Does skin form a barrier against pathogens?

Answer the question: I think that skin _____
_____.

Form a hypothesis: Skin (does/does not) form a barrier against pathogens.

Test the hypothesis:

Materials
- 2 ripe (but not overripe) bananas in their peels
- 2 paper plates

Procedure
- Leave one banana in its peel, and place it on a plate. Unpeel the other banana, and place it on the other plate.
- Observe the bananas for two days and note any changes. After two days, unpeel the banana on the first plate and compare the two pieces of fruit.

Observations: The banana with the peel continued to ripen and may have begun to show signs of rotting. The unpeeled banana rotted quickly.

Conclusions: Skin does form a barrier against pathogens. The skin on the banana kept pathogens in the air from reaching the fruit inside, thereby slowing down the rotting process. Without a skin, the banana was exposed to the pathogens in the air, which began attacking the fruit immediately, speeding up the rotting process. The same is true of skin on the human body, which keeps pathogens from getting inside to cause infection or illness.

Attack and Defend

chapter three

When a harmful invader manages to get by the body's protective barriers, the rest of the immune system steps in.

White Blood Cells

When a foreign visitor arrives inside the body, white blood cells are waiting. These cells patrol the bloodstream and the spaces between body tissues in search of invaders. Some white blood cells will attack anything that doesn't belong in the body. Others attack only certain types of trespassers.

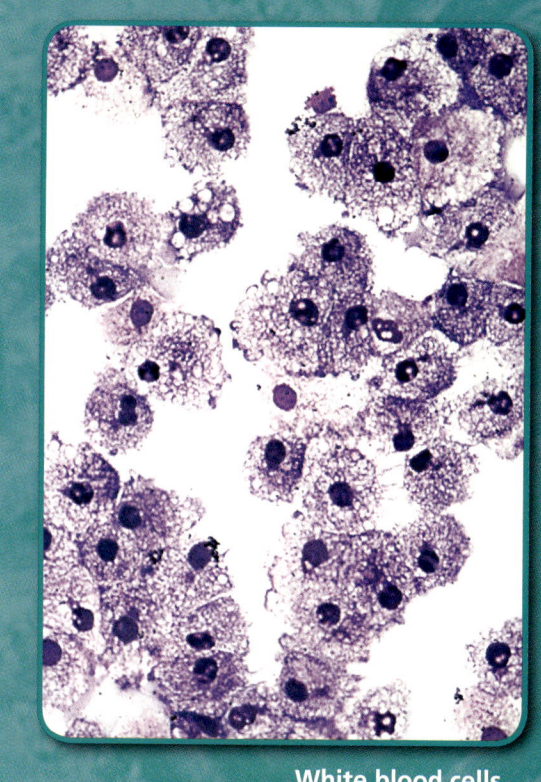

White blood cells

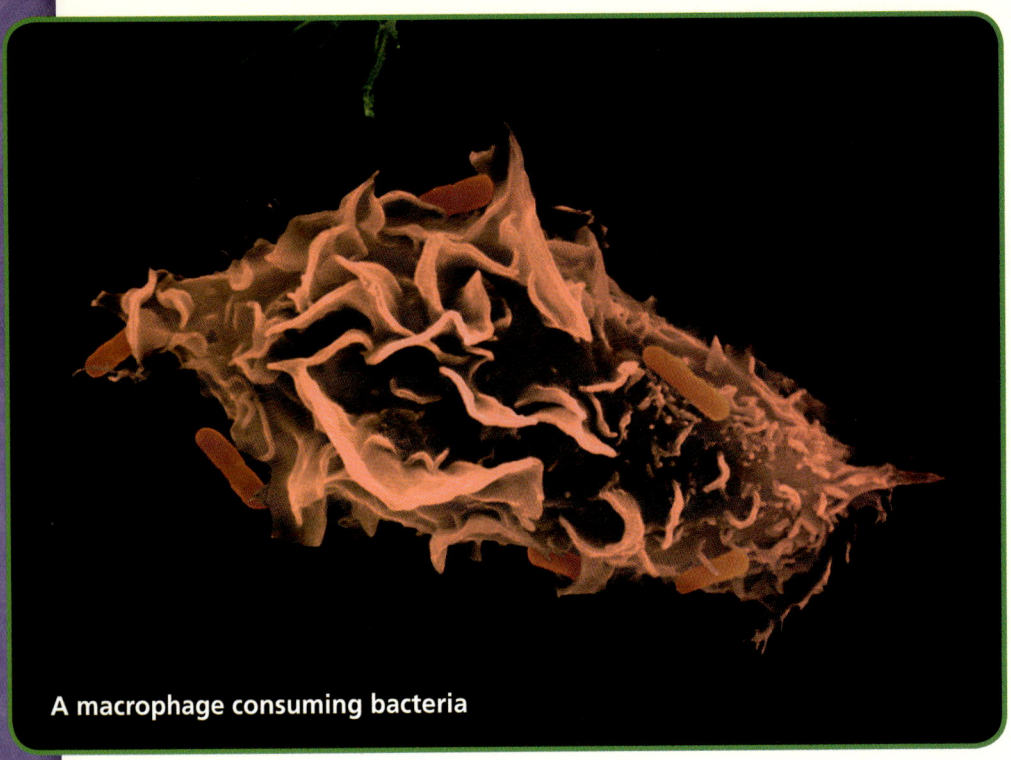
A macrophage consuming bacteria

Macrophages are one of the white blood cells that devour cellular debris and anything that appears to be foreign. *Macrophage* means "big eater." If a macrophage finds something it doesn't recognize, it engulfs and digests it. Macrophages tend to patrol the skin, mucous membranes, and other places where intruders are commonly found.

Proteins, Lysozymes, and Histamines

Antimicrobial **proteins** also protect against pathogen invasion. *Antimicrobial* means "against tiny organisms." These proteins trigger responses to pathogens, helping the body get rid of them before they can cause bigger problems. For example, some antimicrobial proteins signal the body to develop a fever. Higher temperatures inhibit bacterial growth and speed up immune system response and healing.

Lysozymes are **enzymes** found in tears, saliva, and sweat. These enzymes break down the cell walls of some bacteria, helping destroy them.

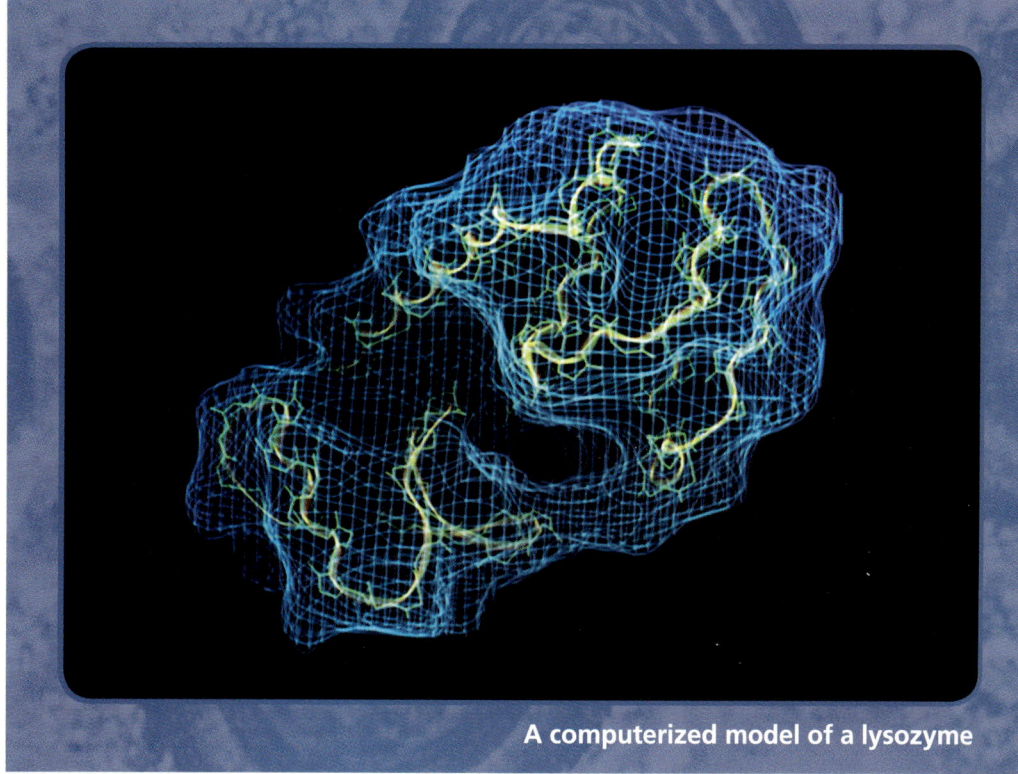

A computerized model of a lysozyme

Histamines are chemicals that direct parts of the body to fight off infection. Histamines tell tissues to collect fluids, causing **inflammation**. Inflammation prevents infections from spreading to neighboring tissue. When tissues in the nose swell, they increase mucus production. This helps capture and wash away bacteria and viruses. Unfortunately, inflammation also causes a sensation of pain or discomfort. So the next time you have a cold, remember that the runny nose, sneezing, and body aches are signs that your immune system is doing its job.

T Cells and B Cells

People who have had chicken pox once rarely get it again, even if they're exposed to the disease. Why? Because their immune system can recognize and destroy the chicken pox virus if it reappears. T cells and **B cells** are the major players in this part of the immune system. These cells form a special group of white blood cells called **lymphocytes**. The majority of mature lymphocytes are found in the lymphoid organs.

After a macrophage engulfs a pathogen, it displays pieces of the pathogen (its antigens) on its surface. When the macrophage introduces the antigens to the correct T cells, an immune system response is triggered.

T cell

A helper T cell (blue) activates a killer T cell (purple), which then attacks a cancer cell (red).

There are two main types of T cells—helpers and killers. Helper T cells identify antigens on "presenter" cells like macrophages. Once activated, helper T cells release chemicals that increase the number and activity of macrophages, killer T cells, and B cells. The killer T cells are designed to destroy infected or cancerous cells.

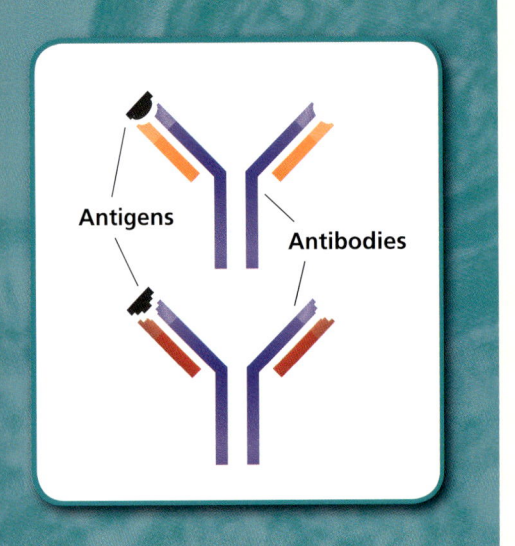

Antigens Antibodies

B cells circulate through the bloodstream and lymphatic vessels. Many gather in the spleen and lymph nodes to search for antigens there. The B cells' main job is to produce ongoing immunity for the body. They do this by producing **antibodies**. Antibodies are small Y-shaped proteins that are specially designed to stick to specific antigens, such as the ones on the virus that cause chicken pox. The antibodies make it harder for the pathogens to invade other cells and spread throughout the body. They also mark the pathogens, making it easier for macrophages and other white blood cells to find and destroy them.

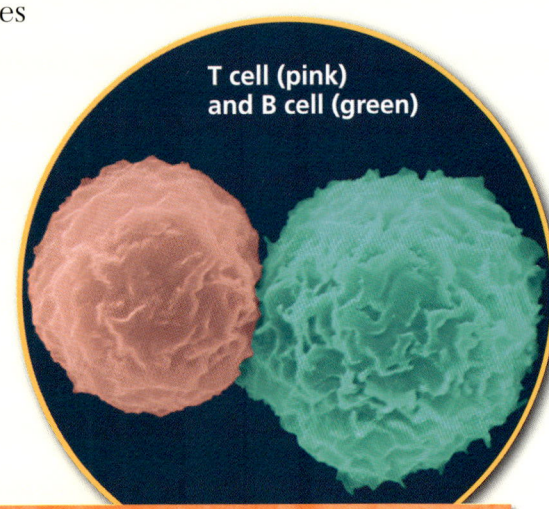

T cell (pink) and B cell (green)

B Is for Bone and T Is for Thymus

Having trouble remembering the difference between B cells and T cells? Try these alphabetical reminders. B cells mature in the **b**one marrow. They are responsible for producing anti**b**odies. T cells mature in the **t**hymus gland. They a**tt**ack pathogens on their **t**urf.

18

Before the invasion is over, another type of B cell is produced. Memory B cells remember the antigen on the invader and store information about making antibodies for it. Memory B cells live for a long time, maintaining a small army of antibodies for a specific disease. This makes it faster and easier for a body to fight off the disease the next time it's exposed to it.

B cells aren't the only cells that form memory cells. T cells also produce memory cells to improve the response to the next exposure of a pathogen.

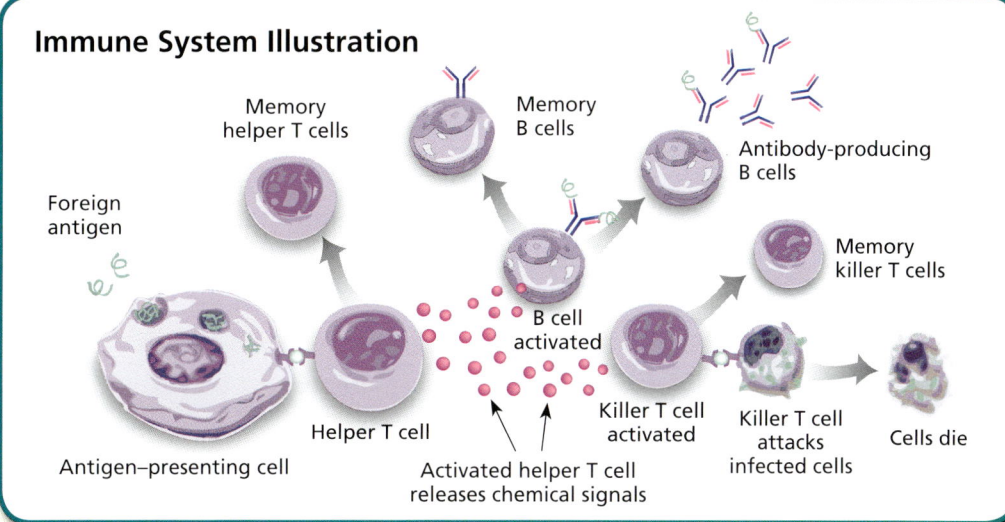

Innate Versus Acquired

Certain aspects of the immune system are present at birth. Others are acquired as you grow and are exposed to pathogens in the environment. Protective features such as skin, macrophage cells, and antimicrobial proteins are part of your innate (born with) immune system. The adaptive, or acquired, immune system is the network of cells, including T cells and B cells, that identify and memorize specific invaders and create antibodies to fight them off if they return.

chapter four

Immunization: Helping Out the Immune System

Long ago, some illnesses and diseases outwitted people's immune systems. Epidemics of the flu, measles, smallpox, and other diseases struck communities, killing hundreds or thousands of people. Then in the 18th century, the discovery of **immunization** provided humans with a way to help their immune systems protect them.

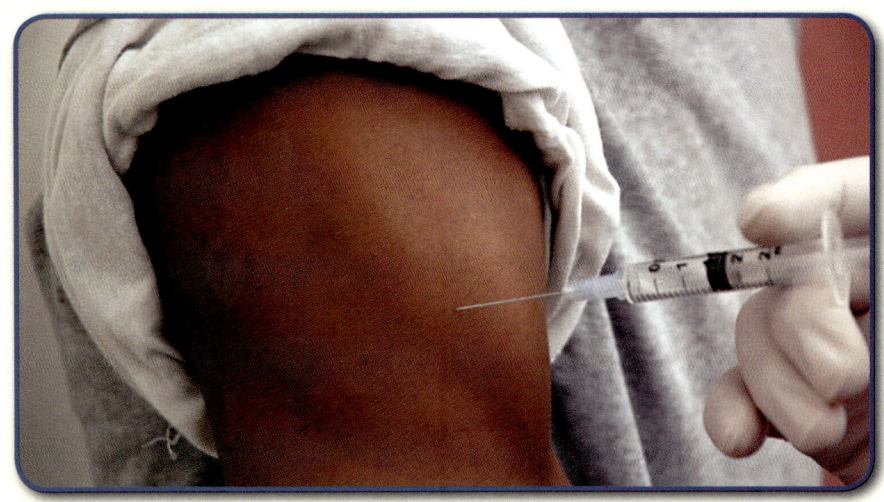

Tracing the Path of Science

In 1718, in the city of Constantinople (now part of Turkey), Lady Mary Wortley Montague witnessed doctors giving patients a mild case of smallpox by rubbing liquid from smallpox blisters into cuts on the patients' hands. The patients developed a mild case of smallpox, recovered, and never had smallpox again. Europeans called the procedure *variolation*.

Lady Montague knew how deadly smallpox could be and recognized the importance of finding a cure. So she decided to test the variolation procedure on her own son. A surgeon named Charles Maitland made a small cut on the child's hand and rubbed in liquid from smallpox blisters. The boy developed a light case of smallpox but quickly recovered. When Lady Montague returned to England, she had her daughter treated too. Maitland also returned to England and tested variolation on six convicted prisoners. All of the treatments were successful.

But variolation was not a perfect procedure. Unhealthy people died when treated with variolation-induced smallpox. And even healthy people sometimes came down with severe cases.

In 1796, Edward Jenner, a country doctor in England, tried a different procedure. Jenner was familiar with country folklore that said that milkmaids who had cowpox never came down with smallpox. Cowpox was a less serious disease similar to smallpox that could be gotten by milking cows. Jenner reasoned that giving a person cowpox using a procedure similar to variolation would protect the person against smallpox.

Jenner tested his hypothesis in May of 1796. Sarah Nelmes, a milkmaid with cowpox, and a boy named James Phipps took part in the experiment. Jenner took some liquid from a blister on Nelmes' hand and rubbed it into scratches on Phipps's arms. The boy developed a fever but soon recovered. Jenner then injected Phipps with smallpox. The boy didn't develop smallpox, seemingly proving that he was now immune to the disease.

Jenner continued his testing for years, calling his procedure *vaccination*, from the Latin word *vacca*, which means "cow." Later this term was used to refer to vaccination against any disease.

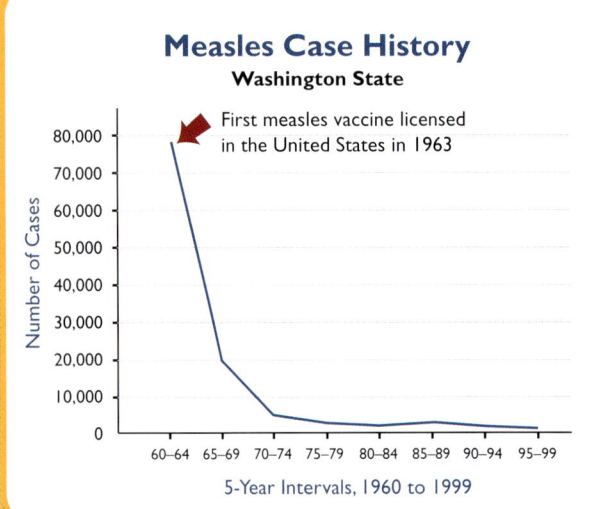

Measles Case History
Washington State

First measles vaccine licensed in the United States in 1963

5-Year Intervals, 1960 to 1999

The experiments with variolation and vaccination were the first documented scientific studies on immunization. Immunization is the process of producing immunity through the use of human-made medicines. Today, most children in developed nations are routinely vaccinated against a variety of diseases that once killed many people.

Like variolation, modern vaccinations work by introducing disease-causing pathogens into the human body. Unlike variolation, however, today's vaccinations use weakened or killed bacteria or viruses. When a **vaccine** is injected into the body, the immune system recognizes the pathogen and fights it off. The immune system also remembers the pathogen in the vaccine, so if a person is exposed to the live form again, the immune system responds quickly, conquering it before it can produce any symptoms.

Vaccines are available for measles, rubella, mumps, tetanus, and many other diseases. However, some diseases still elude modern science. There is no vaccine for the common cold, for example, because the illness is caused by many different viruses that mutate, or change, quickly.

Scientist of Significance

In the 1920s, an outbreak of polio plagued America. Polio is a viral disease that can cause muscle deterioration and paralysis. Jonas Salk was the man responsible for developing a vaccine for this disease.

Salk began his research on polio at the University of Pittsburgh in 1947. At the time, scientists studied the virus by infecting monkeys. By 1949, Salk had developed a technique for growing the virus in cell cultures instead of monkeys. He then developed a polio vaccine by using the chemical formaldehyde to break apart the virus particles so that they could no longer cause infections. He first tested the vaccine on monkeys. Then he tested it on volunteer patients, his own family, and himself. These first tests were promising.

In 1954, about one million children were vaccinated in the first national polio vaccine trial. In 1955, the results of the trial showed that the vaccine was safe and effective. Just two years after the vaccine's release, polio rates in the United States dropped by nearly 90 percent.

After conquering polio, Salk spent years looking for a vaccine for AIDS. Unfortunately, he was not successful in finding one before his death in 1995.

chapter five

Breakdowns in the System

The immune system is a powerful defense against harmful invaders. But sometimes a system fails to function correctly, or it may actually attack the body it's supposed to defend. When this happens, a person's immunity is compromised.

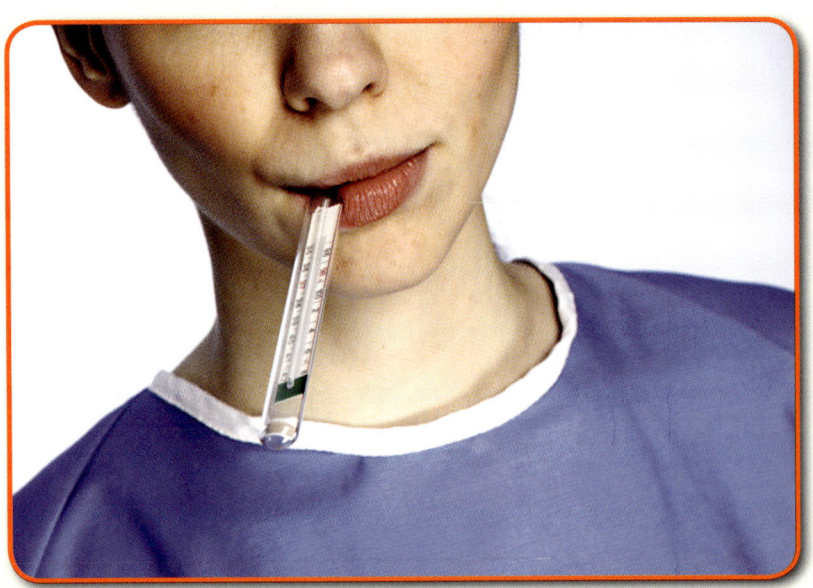

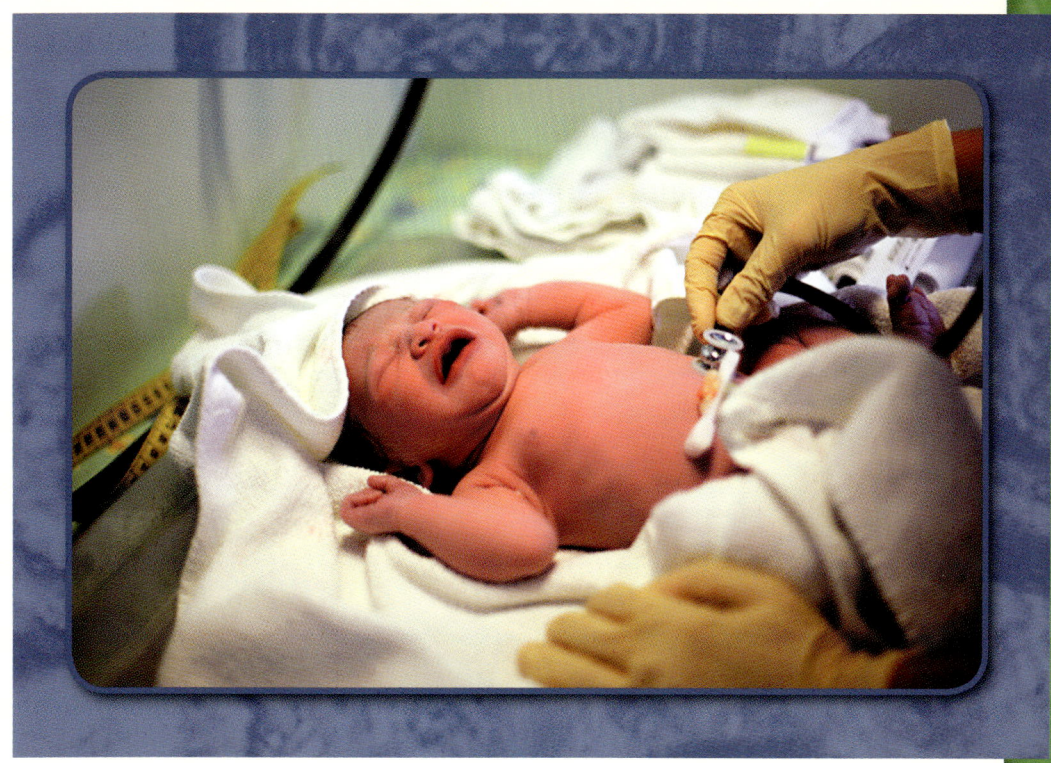

Immunodeficiency Disorders

Immunodeficiency disorders occur when a person's immune system doesn't work correctly. Some of these disorders are present at birth. Others are acquired through events such as exposure to a virus or treatment with certain drugs.

Severe Combined Immunodeficiency Disease (SCIDS) is one immunodeficiency disorder that babies are born with. Children with SCIDS have a severe lack of B cells and T cells. Because of this, they can't fight off even common infections and illnesses.

Another immunodeficiency disorder present at birth is DiGeorge syndrome. Children with DiGeorge syndrome are born without a fully functioning thymus gland (or with no gland at all). Therefore, they don't produce enough mature T cells to help them kill pathogens in the body.

Acquired immunodeficiency syndrome (AIDS) is an acquired disorder. It is caused by the human immunodeficiency virus (HIV). HIV attacks cells of the immune system so it can't respond to infections. This leaves people who are infected with HIV vulnerable to rare cancers, pneumonia, and other infections.

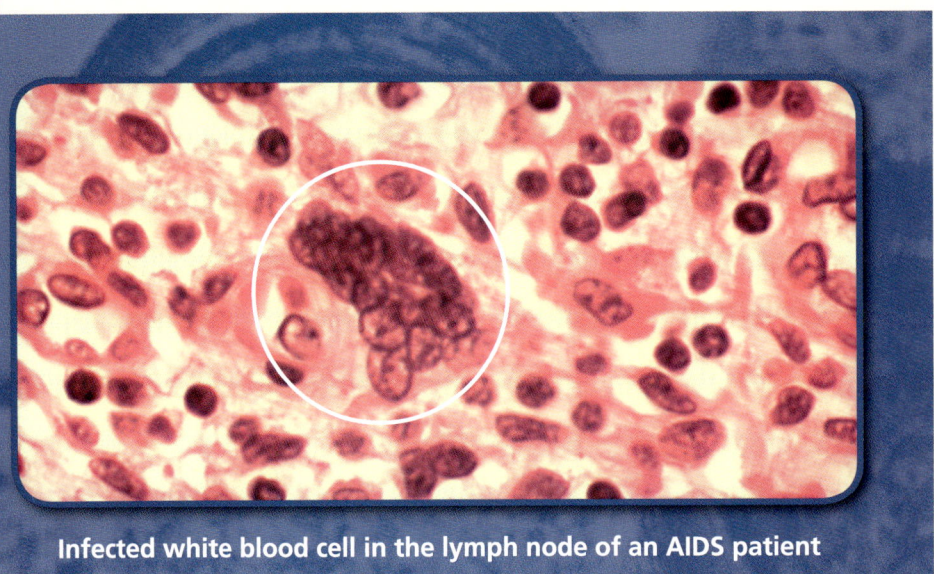

Infected white blood cell in the lymph node of an AIDS patient

Immunodeficiencies can also be acquired as a result of chemotherapy. Chemotherapy is a drug treatment for cancer patients. While the drugs are helpful in killing cancer cells, they also kill healthy cells in the process. When too many cells in bone marrow and other parts of the immune system are killed, the patient's immune system is threatened.

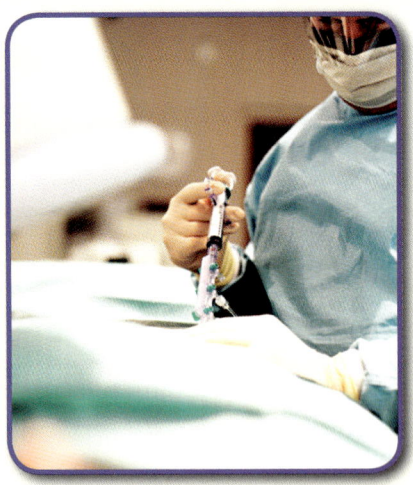

Chemotherapy treatment

More than 2 million Americans suffer from rheumatoid arthritis. About three-fourths of them are women.

Autoimmune Disorders

In some cases, an immune system mistakenly attacks a person's own body, resulting in an autoimmune disorder. Rheumatoid arthritis is an autoimmune disorder in which the immune system attacks a body's joints, causing pain, swelling, and difficulty of movement. People with multiple sclerosis have an immune system that attacks their nerves, resulting in symptoms such as fatigue, numbness, blurred vision, and loss of balance and muscle coordination. Crohn's disease is characterized by stomach pain, nausea, and diarrhea caused by the immune system's attack on the lining of the intestines. Lupus is an autoimmune disorder that can affect organs, joints, and skin.

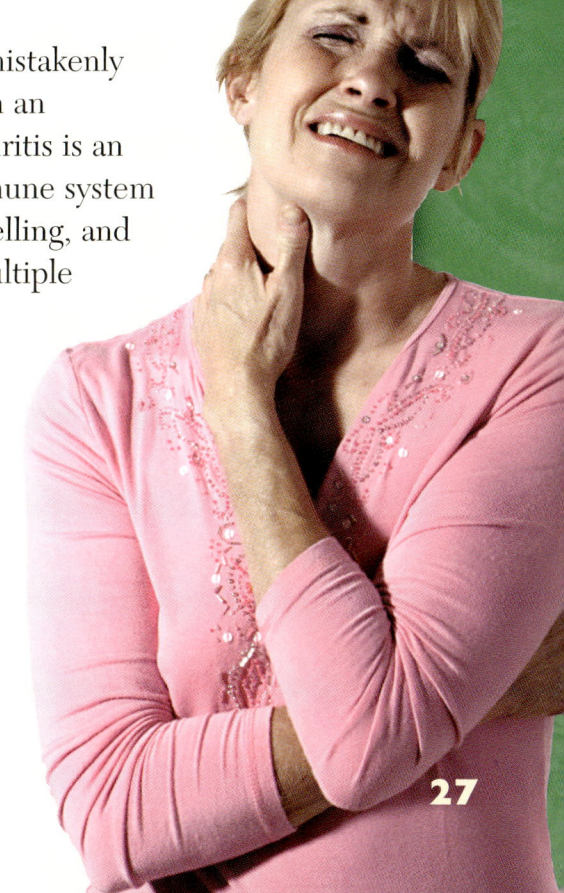

Technology Link

Diagnosing autoimmune disorders is difficult because early symptoms are often vague. Medical technicians have to test each suspected antigen separately to see if it's causing the patient's symptoms. Each test can take days. Antigen microarrays, however, can help doctors diagnose autoimmune diseases much faster.

An antigen microarray is a small glass slide dotted with thousands of proteins and other molecules commonly attacked in autoimmune diseases. A sample of a patient's blood is applied to the microarray. Antibodies in the blood attach themselves to any proteins that are under attack in the patient's body. The technician then applies a fluorescent dye to the antibodies. When the microarray is scanned with a laser, the dye-tagged antibodies glow. The technician can immediately see which proteins are affected.

A single microarray can test for reactions to thousands of possible antigens at once, greatly reducing diagnosis time. Scientists also hope that in the future, microarrays can be used to develop antigen-specific treatments.

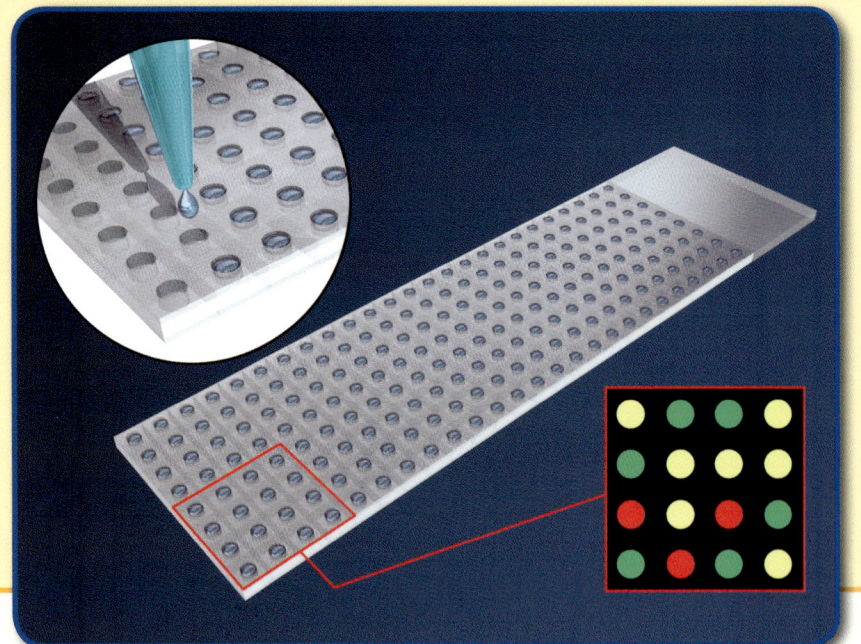

Allergies

Allergies are a result of a body's overreaction to materials in the environment. Even though pollen, peanuts, and bee stings are normally harmless, bodies with allergies respond as though they are threats to the immune system.

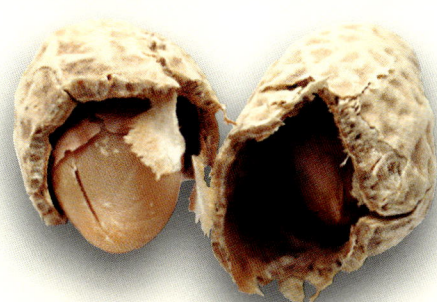

Every time a person with allergies comes in contact with an allergy trigger, or **allergen**, his or her B memory cells remember the material and produce antibodies to fight it off.

Actions Against Allergies

One common treatment for allergies is antihistamines. Antihistamines are drugs that subdue an immune system reaction caused by histamines. Another treatment involves injecting patients with small amounts of an allergen in an attempt to build a tolerance for it. This is a type of immunotherapy.

Transplant Troubles

When organs such as the liver or kidneys fail, they can be replaced by organs from another body. The immune system, however, actually hinders this process. When a body receives a new organ, its immune system doesn't recognize the new tissue. Therefore, the system attacks the new organ. The problem can be helped by finding closely matching tissue and by using drugs to keep the immune system from attacking. However, suppressing the immune system leaves the patient more vulnerable to pathogens, often leading to other complications.

New Investigations into the Immune System

chapter six

The immune system plays a crucial role in the health of all human beings. Scientists are continually studying this complex system to understand how it works, to find new cures and preventions for diseases, and to keep people healthy in their day-to-day lives.

New Hope for Autoimmune Diseases

A new form of treatment for autoimmune diseases is currently in the testing phase. Stem cell treatment may help people with diseases such as rheumatoid arthritis, multiple sclerosis, and lupus. Stem cell treatment involves replacing "faulty" mature cells in the immune system with bone marrow stem cells that can develop into healthy cells.

Stem cells grown in a lab

Researchers at the Northwestern University Medical School are working on a stem cell treatment for lupus. The immune cells in lupus patients attack the body's connective tissue. Connective tissue is found throughout the body in bones, tendons, ligaments, and blood.

During stem cell treatments, doctors extract stem cells from the patient's bone marrow. They grow these cells in a lab while the patient is treated with drugs that destroy the remaining immune cells. The bone marrow stem cells are then returned to the patient's body, where they manufacture new immune cells that don't attack the patient's connective tissue. So far, these treatments have been successful and offer hope to patients with lupus and other autoimmune disorders.

Stressing Out About the Immune System

Does stress increase the chances you'll get sick? Yes, it does, according to numerous studies done by the scientific medical community. Many research teams have proven that too much emotional or physical stress can decrease the functioning of the immune system, leading to an increase in illness.

Two recent studies support this hypothesis. At the University of Wisconsin-Madison, a group of volunteers practiced relaxing meditation for eight weeks. A control group did not meditate and went about their regular routines. After two months, both groups were given a flu vaccine. Blood samples were then taken after a month and again after two months.

The samples showed that the people who had meditated produced stronger antibody responses to the vaccine than the people who had not meditated.

In another study at the University of Chicago, a research team found that bacteria called *Pseudomonas aeruginosa* can turn deadly in bodies that are under physical stress. Pseudomonas bacteria can live harmlessly in the intestines of healthy people. But if people who are carrying these bacteria have surgery, the bacteria can tell the body is stressed and they become dangerous. To study this phenomenon, researchers isolated chemicals produced by lab-grown T cells stimulated to battle infection. They then added these chemicals to a sample of Pseudomonas bacteria. The bacteria had been altered to glow green when they turn infectious. One of the chemicals from the T cells caused the bacteria to glow. This same chemical was known to stimulate cells to fight off bacteria. It appears that if the bacteria encounter this chemical in a body, they know the immune system is gearing up to fight off potentially harmful invaders. The Pseudomonas bacteria see this as a threat and fight back, becoming dangerous.

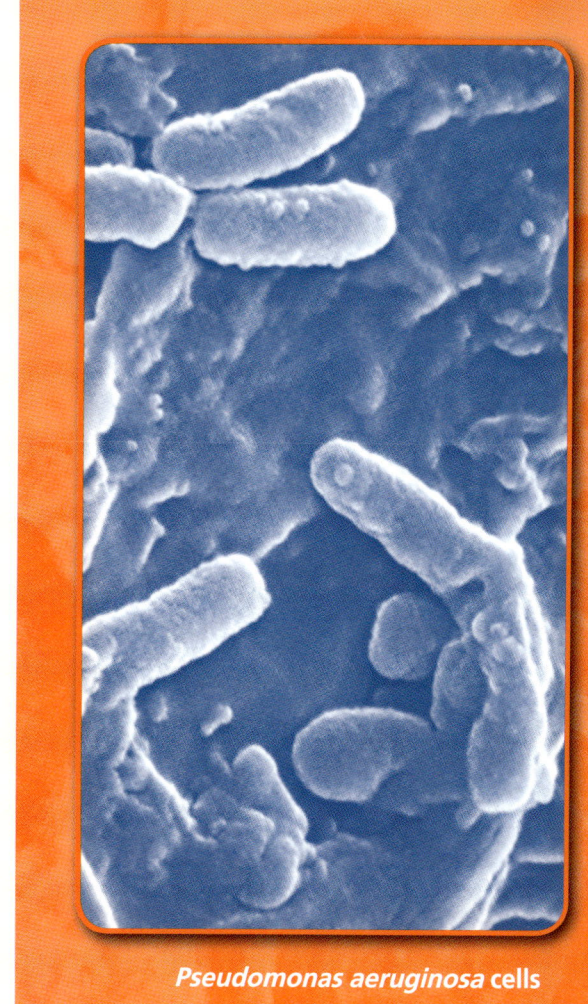

Pseudomonas aeruginosa **cells**

What's the message in these and other studies about stress and its effects on the immune system? While a certain amount of stress can be helpful in revving up your system, too much stress can actually threaten your immune system. So finding ways to keep your stress under control will keep you happy and healthy.

Herbal Solutions?

Many people take herbal supplements to improve various aspects of their health. But is there an herb that specifically helps boost the immune system? It was once thought so, but studies are now showing that may be debatable.

Health food stores sell a variety of forms of echinacea, an herb that has been reported to strengthen the immune system. However, recent studies in the United States suggest that the herb may not be doing anything for the immune system. One study conducted at the University of Virginia involved nearly 400 young adults. Some of the volunteers were given a liquid dose of echinacea, while those in the control group were given an identical-looking liquid that contained no echinacea. After taking their liquids for a week, the volunteers were given nasal sprays containing cold viruses. They were then confined to hotel rooms for five days to avoid encountering other viruses. Those who were taking echinacea continued to take it. Half of the volunteers in the control group were now given echinacea, while the others continued taking the nonherbal liquid. Regardless of whether they took echinacea before or after the infection or not at all, about three-fifths of the volunteers developed colds with similar symptoms. Blood tests from all three groups showed no difference in the production of antibodies or any other chemicals produced by the immune system.

The debate is ongoing. Some doctors and researchers are sticking to their original claims that echinacea supports the immune system. Others have yet to be convinced. Perhaps future studies will prove once and for all whether taking echinacea is a solution to improving the immune system.

* * *

While scientists continue to investigate and debate ways to heal or improve the body's immune system, one thing they all agree on is the system's importance to the body. The immune system is the body's first and foremost line of defense against the harmful invaders that surround it every day. A strong, healthy immune system is the key to a strong, healthy you!

Internet Connections for the Immune System

http://health.howstuffworks.com/immune-system.htm

Find out how your immune system works, how it can malfunction, and what you can do to help it defend your body.

http://kidshealth.org/parent/general/body_basics/immune.html

This KidsHealth overview of the immune system discusses the roles, members, and disorders of the body's defense system.

http://www.immunisation.nhs.uk/article.php?id=71

Explore the science of immunity and vaccines. Then click on "History" to trace the path of vaccination through time.

http://www.metrokc.gov/health/immunization/system.htm

Find out how immunization helps activate your immune system and prevents you from getting certain illnesses.

Glossary

allergen (AL er jen) material that causes the immune system to overreact in allergies

antibody (AN ti bah dee) protein produced by B cells that binds to pathogens, stopping them from harming a body

antigen (AN ti jen) chemical marker on a foreign substance in a body that provokes an immune system response

B cell (bee sel) type of white blood cell that produces antibodies

bacteria (bak TEAR ee uh) single-celled organisms without a nucleus, some of which cause illness or infection in the human body

cell (sel) smallest unit of life

enzyme (EN zeyem) protein that causes chemical reactions inside a cell to occur more quickly

histamine (HIST uh meen) chemical that causes irritation, muscle contraction, and swelling in an attempt to fight off pathogens

immunity (im YOU nuh tee) body's ability to resist illness or disease

immunization (im you nuh ZAY shuhn) process of making someone resistant, or immune, to an illness or disease by giving him or her a vaccine

inflammation (in fluh MAY shuhn) swelling, redness, heat, and pain produced in an area of the body as a reaction to injury or infection

lymph node (limf nohd) oval body that houses and produces white blood cells and filters harmful organisms out of the fluid in lymphatic vessels

lymphatic vessel (lim FAT ik VES uhl) tube that transports lymph fluid to the bloodstream

lymphocyte	(LIM fuh seyet) one of a group of white blood cells that fight off pathogens in a body
lysozyme	(LEYE suh zeyem) enzyme that causes some bacteria to break down
macrophage	(MAK ruh fayj) white blood cell that kills pathogens in a body
organ	(OR guhn) group of tissues that work together to perform a job in the body; independent body part
pathogen	(PATH uh jen) organism or virus that can cause disease or infection in a body
protein	(PROH teen) large molecule made by cells that helps with their growth, repair, and replacement
red bone marrow	(red bohn MAR oh) reddish jellylike substance inside some bones that makes red and white blood cells
spleen	(spleen) lymphoid organ that houses and produces white blood cells and filters blood
stem cell	(stem sel) cell that can divide to replace itself and to produce specialized cells
T cell	(tee sel) type of white blood cell that fights pathogens in a body
thymus gland	(THEYE muhs gland) organ where white blood cells mature into T cells
tissue	(TISH you) group of similar cells working together
vaccine	(vak SEEN) medicine made of weakened, dead, or broken up bacteria or viruses that produces an immune response
virus	(VEYE ruhs) tiny particle that infects and reproduces inside the cells of organisms
white blood cell	(weyet bluhd sel) type of blood cell that fights infections and diseases

Index

adaptive (acquired) immune system, 19
allergies, 29
antibodies, 18–19, 28
antigens, 5, 16, 17, 18, 28
autoimmune disorders, 27, 28, 30, 31
herbal remedies for the immune system, 34–36
immune system
    adenoids, 8
    antimicrobial proteins, 14
    appendix, 8
    histamines, 15
    lymph nodes, 6, 18
    lymphatic vessels, 6, 18
    lysozymes, 15
    macrophage cells, 14, 16, 17, 18
    mucous membranes, 11
    Peyer's patches, 8
    red bone marrow, 7
    saliva, 11
    skin, 10, 12
    spleen, 8, 18
    stomach acids, 11
    sweat, 11

immune system *continued*
    tears, 11
    thymus gland, 8, 18
    tonsils, 8
    white blood cells, 7, 13
        B cells, 16, 17, 18–19, 29
        T cells, 8, 16, 17, 18, 19, 33
immunity, 9
immunization, 20–23
immunodeficiency disorders, 25–26
innate immune system, 19
Jenner, Edward, 21
lymphocytes, 16
Maitland, Charles, 21
microarrays, 28
Montague, Mary Wortley, 21
organ transplants, 29
pathogens (definition), 7
Salk, Jonas, 23
stem cell treatments, 30–31
stress and the immune system, 9, 32–34
vaccination, 21, 22
variolation, 21, 22